Eden Waters Press

# HOME

## Anthology

edited by Anne Brudevold

HOME

| | |
|---|---|
| Editor | Anne Brudevold |
| Contributing Editors | Katherine Adams |
| | Jim Foritano |
| | Liz Watson |
| Production editor | Steve Glines |
| cover photo | Erik Iversen |


ISBN 978-0-6151-8243-8

EDEN WATERS is published once a year. We publish poems, short fiction and address a different theme for each issue. We welcome submissions from June 1-September 30. All material must be previously unpublished. *EDEN WATERS PRESS edits and publishes books and chapbooks year around. For chapbooks, please send a draft. For books, send a query letter and a summary.*

Thank you to the Bagel Bards, especially Doug Holder, for support, good humor, and spreading the word. Thanks to everyone who submitted work to us. We were overwhelmed by submissions, and had to reject some excellent manuscripts, because we simply didn't have room. Thanks to each and every one of you who submitted.

Eden Waters Press
16 Harcourt St.
The Residences @Copley Place,Apt.2B
Boston, 02116
http://edenwaterspress.com

Eden Waters Press

# HOME
# Anthology

Anne Brudevold

Each day the miracle of emptiness,
the whirlwind that sings up the world.
You say you know the blessings of its presence,
but with what do you build your home?

translated by Kevin Bowen and
Nguyen Ba Chung, from

Zen Master
Chan Khong (Vuong Hai Thiem)
(1016-1100)

From poems of early Vietnam, colleted by Nugyen Duy, used by permission

# Contents

Anne Brudevold

*Iris Dunkle*

## What Falls from the Sky

*1*

When my brother and I flew the kite
we thought it was an experiment in weather.
Each of us fought to follow the cord out
and up, giving more line, until finally
we had to tie it to the farthest corner
of the barbed wire fence. That night, the storm claimed it.

At school, when we were given balloons,
they were explained to us as expressions of love—
we were told to tie messages to their strings—let them go
in hopes, that when the balloons fell
from the sky, someone would find our messages.

My brother and I already knew
no one would find our messages—
love is what lifts up and leaves.

*2*

I don't remember where I was first marked
to stand. But my brother and I quietly studied
and then assumed the roles of extras in the house.

I was convinced my mother was dying.
She stood so often at the silver sink, washing dishes,
her hands were pink and raw. Sometimes
she'd even wash my hair in it silver
(her hair she painted red
because only children should contain their age.)

When she stayed in bed for a week
part of me remained by her bedside, praying,
(that's the part of me that was her);
the other part (my father) had already left.

*3*

The hot-air balloon happened like a miracle.
I don't remember it landing
by accident in the backyard,
but after, there were cars everywhere—
men in the fields gathering yards and yards
of the balloon's silk shining cloth
in their out-stretched arms.

Then, out from the basket spilled
a man, a wife, still dressed for their wedding
as if they had just fallen off a cake.

And all afternoon, the house shifted with their weight
as their laughter colored the dark house bright.

After they left, I found the rings at the sink—
two gold bands, shining in the soap dish.

The house had become even larger than before—
my brother and I, pacing in order to fill it,
agreed, the rings were not a message, but a curse.

*4*
The trick of memory is—it fills itself out:

My father has returned.
It is raining.
How small he looks standing
in the gape of the open door,
like a wet bird.
He smiles at my brother, at me
at my mother lingering behind us.
He's holding flowers
as if he's brought spring itself.
And the curtain falls over the whole house.

It doesn't lift for years.

Anne Brudevold

*Paul Hotovsky*

## House Over the World

This morning over breakfast
my daughter tells me her dream
of long division. At first

she's sailing through a math test,
jumbles of numbers swelling and breaking
gently down all around her,
the stalwart rudder of her number 2 pencil
steering her steadfastly through.

Then out of nowhere a word problem:
*The house over the world.*
A fraction the shape of an iceberg.
She can't simplify and she can't
tack. She can only

watch as the house turns into *our* house,
and the dream turns into the nightmare
of our house divided by the world.
The world into our house
how many times?

*Daniel Varoujan translated by Diana Der-Hovanessian*

## Coming Home

*In 1915, 250 poets were rounded up, imprisoned, then killed by the Ottoman Turks before the genocide of the rest of the Armenian population in Turkey. (Poets were considered leaders and dangerous.) This poem was written by Daniel Varoujan during the months he was in prison before he was executed. His notebook, ransomed by one of his guards to an Armenian priest, contained this poem about students coming home for the spring holidays.*

We're coming home tonight, singing together,
coming home by white moonlight.
O village houses, O you village houses,
wake up all the dogs in all the yards.
Wake up all the wells and fountains and
let them bubble up to fill our pitchers.
We're bringing flowers, flowers for the holidays.
And we're singing, we come singing of love.
We're coming by the mountain road,
houses, o you houses. Open the gates now
as the oxen horns push them in.
Let the oven's smoke rise to mix
with the blue smoke of the roofs.
And you shy young wives of the houses,
with new babies, bring milk in blue
clay pitchers. We're coming home.

*Philip Burnham*

## Before You Left

Before you left, all the kitchen cupboards
Were filled with honey sweet and savory
Provisions of your absent love, stored,
Too, in pine bureau drawers, carefully
Laid out on soft linens' pillow cases,
Draped over closet hangers' patient frames
Set forever in familiar faces
Smiled from a gathered crowd of pictured names,
Found in the arms of comfortable chairs,
Glazed on the circles of our dinner plates,
Hidden as random sighs on wooden stairs,
Wound up within the clock's tock-tocking gait
Making a measure of your lost presence
Whose souvenirs linger in affection
To surround my living as an incense
That burns and smolders its way to heaven.

*Joyce Nower*

## Humble Skills

Humble skills. Patience polished into
learned naturalness, I practiced hands cupped
catching water from the bathroom tap.

My small fingers finally formed a sealed hollow,
a pool to reflect an eye, to see one day
sky well up over rock and water, a system.

Years later, biking near a Vermont town
I stopped by icy pools of water formed
in polished rock like rounded bowls worn down

by endless invisible streams that slaked the thirst
of sycamores and pines ranging the mountains.
I knelt down and cupped my hands to drink.

*Jill Winkowski*

## tremor

I am shaken
to my foundation
a seven on the Richter scale
feeling the tremors rocking
buildings crash down
bunk beds
cabinets crumble
china plates break in half

in the aftermath
i walk up a slanted floor
to a cracked window
i look out and see
all the lifeless bodies
on the asphalt
i gape at my worried fingertips
ask myself,
can this be my blood?

*Jim Foritano*

## Invitation

Hard to think of simply as a birdhouse,
as I stepped off the sidewalk—a pedestrian focused on home.

Weathered to the same color and texture
of the scuffed bark of which it seemed a second part.

Worth another look to know further
how simplicity grows in the mind of the maker.

Is it the in-dweller, or the tree giving cues?

What tells us to stop or continue
so that what we make is a luminous summons?

As I crossed old streets, I came home to that house;
shook off new feathers from the damp and the cold,

entered as a few ounces of weight
on dainty feet.

*Liz Watson*

## Turning the Page

What is it that eats
upon my days?
Wrinkles skin
gnaws away at dreams,
surges, like life diminishing
through pipes of pink sinew
with indulgent ways.

Could I capture her
like a star from the milky breast
of the southern night?
Hide her in that ceramic cherub
I place upon my bathroom vanity.
Withhold her breath,
her rhythm in the night
the bellows emptied, left.

How can I know her?
Wedged between the pages of
the book a child cries
on leaving...
Tumbling into space
again.

That child lifts off into her future
the mother leaves behind
wheels jammed on the tarmac,
clocks turning back,
devouring all it claims.
And she plays, her dolls
making family games.

The child inside her skin ages,
her life inside the journal
passing with each turning
of the page.

collection of Anne Brudevold

*Andrea Nicki*

## homeless

headache right between my eyes
drills a hole

tree grows between my eyes
somebody else's backyard

street post between my eyes
somebody else's city

flag between my eyes
somebody else's territory

Katherine Adams

*Pam Rosenblatt*

## By the highway

home home home
here by the highway
sleep in tents drink
people don't understand people understand
people want us to leave we want to stay
spring brought us here spring brought us here
here we stay here by the highway
day after  day  night after  night
at dusk  like  raccoons  we  wander
take  what's  rightfully  ours
we live here we live here we live here
tax-free jobless homeless
near the truck repair shop  squatters rights
go away go away go away
highway department  spring brought us here
spring brought us here spring brought us here
here by the highway route 93 off ramp in east somerville.

*Birgit Kvamme Lundheim*

## Sans Domicile Fixe

Will you protect me?
I know I shouldn't ask.
To you I'm just another "I" and yet—
I'm cold.

The tint of your façade—You're made of cardboard,
n'est-ce pas?
I do not mind—you're still a house—a room?

So you're sort of a room? All right, that's fine
with me. A lid between the blacks (that of immensity,
that of an eye) is all I need—no roof,
just walls. I see. So you're a kind of box, then?

Without a bottom, but still a box, on ice. Starfish
and winter stars above and below; a box with a view.

I'm in, I'll stay, I'll do my bit.
Box! I'll see you every day.

*Holly Anderson*

## Bovina, 4 PM

A motherless mob of winds
riding up the northern ridge
scribbled languages
on the billowing meadow.

There's a Braille of ridges and blue divots
while winds from the south erase whole passages
leaving lines in winter light that movė like
hanks of come-hither hair or horse tails.

Three of us tear through reams of fresh snow
rewriting incident by accident
on injection molded squeaking snow shoes
mail-ordered in from Utah

Anne Brudevold

*Barbara Bialick*

## The Play of the Soil is the Play of the Soul

My mother as a child was
playing in the dirt again—she
had sweet soil smeared on
her white Sabbath dress, nice
soft earth that was
so much fun.

But her cousin Fradell was
terified she'd be scolded
by my mother's mother for
dressing the little girl up,
and then letting her out
of the house.

For Mother back then, even
as now, loved to play
with the city dirt
under the porch and on
the grass in
Detroit in the 1920's.

As she grew up she realized one kind
of dirt made her sad, like when
her sister died at 17. Even now
she believes that cemetery sod
is sacred—"It's the actual
eventual home of everyone."

*Tom Sheehan*

## Compensation

Coming home along the river,
clouds hallowing deep blue
pools for phantom trout,
I wait your presentation.

You walk beneath the ash tree,
trash bags bloom in your hands,
a light wind combs your hair
and selects outer strands.

to be August's sole tinsel.
Soft stride presumes darkness
is still about reeds and rushes,
your hips float like two ships

on the bay at tide change.
Toil covets all your time,
thrusts you into worn denim,
shoes braced with solid heels,

demands quick deliverance
of a forgotten bride.
Thread me into your labors,
weave me onto the high day.

collection of Anne Brudevold

*Barbara Beckwith*

## Wild Home

My home is an upper floor apartment of a double-decker in Cambridge MA, population 101,000. My bedroom peers into my neighbor's kitchen. At night, I fall asleep to screeching tires and the rumble of trucks.

I visit the wilderness only a few weeks each summer. But daily I glory in mountain peaks, slickrock canyons, whitewater rapids, alpine gardens, and winter woods.

Each morning, I wake early to walk three miles into Harvard Square and back. I start when the streets are still quiet, the light is low, and the green of my city still glows.

The two-family houses in my neighborhood sit flank to flank, separated only by skinny sideyards. But a block away, I enter a neighborhood of big homes and expansive lawns. These I hurry past with head down: mown lawn to me is barren, lacking the weeds, saplings, and insect life of the meadows I have known and loved.

Further on, I pass a fence that hides a manor-like house. A tangle of rhododendron, laurel and hemlock that serves the owner as a noise buffer, serves me as time travel. The sight of even a short swath of untamed brush takes me back to my Pennsylvania woods, where such bushes grew wild, and where I, as a youngster, picked blueberries, followed deer trails, and kept an eye out for snakes, poison ivy, salamanders, and trees to climb. The tickle of orange lizards in my hand, the stretch of my legs as I reached a tree's highest branch, the heat in my ears as my ten year old self walked a path where a bear was spotted the week before: these all come back. I am here and I am there, as well.

My concrete city sidewalk skirts a corner park with a mini Old Faithful spurting from a stone base. The sight of pulsing water sends my mind careening down New Hampshire's Swift River, jouncing atop the standing waves of the Allagash, steering past humps of water that hide treacherous boulders on the Delaware, and being stared down by a moose on Maine's Dead River, who readied himself to charge but instead urinated long and hard and sauntered away.

I walk below a lovely weeping willow: it leaves me indifferent, carrying no resonance with my past. I pass a garden full of chrysanthemums: their colors please only my eye, not my soul. Waxy white Indian pipe and creamy yucca glow more brightly in my mind from the few times I came upon them in woods or wilderness.

My morning walk ends on "Tory Row"—lower Brattle Street. Here, colonial homes wear blue plaques to certify their historical value. Approaching the Longfellow House, I pass a granite wall. The poet's image does not cross my mind. Instead: a glint of mica, feldspar and quartz grab me and I am back in the Sierra Mountains, where as a teenager, I fell in love with rock. It was then that I first scaled granite peaks despite the thin air and ice that coated my drinking water. My thirst for mountains never slacked: I went on to explore the Rockies, the Cascades, the Wind Rivers, the White Mountains, the volcanoes of Hawaii. Each encounter drifts back at the least provocation: the skunk in my tent, the bear on the trail, the slot canyons, the rainforests, the towering beeplants, the evening primroses that open each morning and closed each night.

The concrete sidewalk under my feet turns to brick. The brickway rises and falls, the result of winter ice heaves: I look down so I won't trip. The red glow puts me in Utah's sandstone canyonlands: the cool of an overhang in 120 degree heat, damp orchids in spring seeps, wind-shaped arches, the pull of quicksand, the prickly brush.

My mind sees sagebrush and cactus, as my body arrives in Harvard Square.

§

*Chad Parenteau*

## Discarded

He's been away for so long,
his unworn gym clothes started smelling
like a workout again, out of boredom.

With the locks changed for reasons
unrelated to him, all he could do
is leave an envelope and a note
asking for the mail that's been coming
here since he's left, putting barely enough
postage to cover the first week's worth.

I wonder if he still hoped
for the broken box he always refused
to leave out for trash day.
Before the purge that his absence allowed,
I opened it, found a top layer of divorce,
stopped when I saw the torn cards
from his former second family.
I discovered that on top of watching
"Good Will Hunting" in his room
until he passed out in front of vodka bottles
of ever-declining price, he would will
the glass inside his picture frames
to split between himself and ex-wife
but never well enough, always losing
something else he needed.

*Doug Holder*

## The Poet's House was Broken In To

They made off
with cheap costume jewelry
a ruin of a laptop
a box
that glittered
but with nothing inside.
All that
I valued
I didn't bother to hide.
My books were undisturbed nor did they
touch
my leather-bound
collected works.
All I could think of was:
What jerks!

New York Skyline
James "BONES" Tomaselli

*Lo Galluccio*

## Here I Am Anyway

*Part I.*

I was fired from a temp job at Morgan Stanley in Times Square about a month before the World Trade Towers were attacked by terrorists in airplanes on the infamous day we now call 9/11. It was the most conservative NY company I had ever worked for and my job was tracking paper for the office who hired temps, screening them with criminal background and drug tests. One day early on I had showed up to work in maroon tights—not a far out color, in fact it's Harvard's emblematic shade—and was told to go down to Duane Reade and pick up some nylons. At the time I was still hooked on a tough beautiful heroin addict in Boston named Freddie who wore CK1. So I bought some of that too. Ostensibly I was fired for surfing the web one day during some down time. It was a part-time job and though the temp agency assured me I'd get another gig, I went down. I couldn't eat for four days and when I finally had breakfast at a restaurant I used to waitress at on Ave B I threw it up after talking to Freddie. It later occurred to me that my connection to him had not served me well in New York City.

I had a good therapist, well competent anyway, at a clinic near Forbes magazine, where I also used to work for the Director of IT. See I was considering beating it back to Boston for a while because I didn't think I could recover from this job loss, the strain of it, my anger about it, the whole ridiculous temp world. Part of me still wanted Freddie. Also, a jazz pianist was interested in making a record with me. And that seemed better than treading water in Babylon. The shrink said, "Well if he's a junkie he loves dope more than you and though home offers some support, you may want to consider staying and fighting in NY and figuring out why you got rejected by the corporate world." Brilliant. Staight ahead. So where was home anyway? I had spent eight years on the Lower East Side in a tiny dark studio apartment that was rent stabilized with a landlord who resembled Cruella Da Ville. I'd made a solo CD called "Being Visited" of which I was fairly proud but it was a no-money deal. Still it meant everything to me and a famous NY DJ had given me some radio play.

Why did Freddie bewitch me? He was through and through a Boston boy. He was a high-school drop out who worked in his Uncle Vito's Auto Body shop. Good in bed but devilish trouble. He looked like Al Pacino's son. Even when I got pregnant by him—and had no intention of bearing his child because neither of us were responsible enough to raise a kid, we had great sex. Those were days of some of the worst sins of my life. Now a shrink was telling me to stand and fight for the City I had come to as an artist with a dream. You know the Dylan song: "She's an artist, she don't look back." That's really what I should have done. Dump the addict and deal.

There is one other twist to the story which may explain why I chose the big black eyed car boy as my lover. Magical psychic voices—cruel and penetrating—had come to me while I was finishing up my record in the studio. They hurt me in my sleep and I was in a lot of pain. Freddie had a bad drug habit but a big Italian heart that hooked me. Sometimes he'd scream at me, "Why don't you just stay here (Boston) so you can have the Italian family you always wanted?" The first night he came, he went straight to St. Mark's Place to cop and I followed him and told the dealers not to sell him dope. I was horrified because I thought he was on methadone and shouldn't be shooting up. I broke down crying on the street. And then I got so mad I wanted to lock him out for the night. It would have been the smart move.

The morning I decided to go home, I'd sublet my place on Ave A and thought it might be a three week sojourn at my mom's house—I had a bottle of Seagram's and some condoms to take back with me. In point of fact, home was a liberal college town where I'd attended a big public high school, lived on a street lined with mansions in an old brick apartment building, my father and my father's death when I was 15, attending Harvard College and then leaving, leaving for acting school in Chicago at 21 and then leaving again home with $2000 borrowed from an old friend of my father's to pursue an acting career in New York that took me to Greece with a LaMama Company. More than that, home was my mother. And we had always had a somewhat strained relationship, despite her clear blue eyes and Betty Crocker timers. Why did I think that I could be an artist living in her house? Why did I think that she and Freddie and this guy who wanted to make a record with me went together? Also, how did it solve the problem of my dreams being altered and the voices? Oh yes, the voices had altered my night-time dreams.

## *Part 2.*

Rolando transforms trash. He was one of the original squatters on the Lower East Side of Manhattan, fighting off the police to take over abandoned buildings. Born near Naples, he has the strong hands and a feel for justice that made him a leader in the struggle. He won a place in a building on 7th street and set up a studio called RAP, Recycle and Pray. After "Being Visited" was finished, in about 1998, I was invited to a party at the squat and fell in love with the way he had decorated it with zebra wall hangings and costumes and colored lights. At the doorway there were hundreds of wine bottles he had sunk in cement that shone in the light at different angles. He invited me to be a guest on his underground radio show where he'd spin my CD and interview me as Queen of Mars, a character from the record. The voices told me he was "special" and as I left the party there was a ringing in my left ear.

The voices would wake me up at night and torment me with messages. They said I was in a fish bowl. I got so angry I smashed my kitchen window three times. When Rolando saw this, he offered to let me stay in the squat with him. There was an extra room and he had a loft bed on the other side of a curtain. We had already made love once I think. It was summer time. He was 17 years older than me but in very good shape—handsome and charming and eccentric. He reminded me of a lone wolf, with white hair and smooth sinewy bones. So I sublet my studio and moved into RAP.

A lot happened during that time, a lot happened because the voices didn't think I was the best partner for Rolando. So they tormented me with jealousy messages. I once threw a bookshelf down a flight of stairs. But I also cleaned all his wine bottles and bought some pink plastic flowers that I hung like a grotto in the bike room. It cleaned the place up. Let me explain this. My voices came from the Hindu deity Ganesha. He was devilishly tricky with me. And because Rolando was a Sufi spirit and into trance music and liked women, Ganesha's voice said I had to pay him a penance. The irony being that Rolando wanted to protect me from these spirits to begin with. Maybe RAP could have been my home, if I had given up my studio and given in to Rolando's often stubborn ways. He wanted to take me to Italy and I tried to help him become more practical as an artist. Actually, he just liked to make things out of aluminum and coffee cans and go on late night excursions to find good trash to use. His soymilk chairs were really cool. In fact the squat had been featured in a NY Times lifestyle section.

This is the backstory. Or part of it. After we finally split up, and Rolando traded RAP for another squat in a building on 3rd Street called "Bullet Space" we gradually became friends.

Where was home then? What could fix my busted up heart? The voices, I think, were gone. But my psyche had been very fucked up. Where is home? It's in your dreams and your energy. It's in your memory and your partnerships. It's in the nest you make with your lovers. It's the past and the future. Isn't it?

*Part 3.*

Okay, I've sublet my place in NY for three weeks. A beautiful black man in Lalita Java coffee shop took my hands in his hands and said, "You're psychic and sensitive and you may think you're going home for a few weeks, but it will be at least 3 months." He also told me that instead of being so obsessed with Freddie's heroin addiction, he would give me "my angel wings' if I wanted. Nothing too dangerous. Just some sniffing. I still said "No." Part of me never wanted to do dope.

Then I'm back at Buckingham St. in my mother's apartment, where I grew up. It is fastidiously organized and clean. She has new furniture she ordered from some company in North Carolina. The only piece I really dig is a captain's desk over which she hangs some Japanese prints. I sleep in my old room, painted white, overlooking the backyard, in a single bed. When 9/11 happens I am so depressed and out of it because a band tour of Italy I had counted on has been cancelled I can barely watch the footage on TV. My little sister chides me, "This is one of the saddest days in America." I can barely get out of bed.

I remember how, as a little girl, I would wake up in the middle of the night convinced my mother was going to come into my bedroom and murder me. I had these night terrors for awhile and never told either of my parents. I could wake my father up when I had nightmares and he would put warm compresses on my legs, sore from ballet classes, but I could never tell him the truth. My subconscious must have projected some jealousy factor onto my mother, some Freudian triangle, because I was always closer to my father. I had never developed a strong emotional bond to my mother, even after my father died. Yet, there I was at 38, back in my old bedroom.

So, there I was stuck between Freddie, my heroin addict lover and my practical, albeit generous and rather controlling mother, who still got up at 6:30 a.m. every morning to work for Harvard/Smithsonian across the street as Chief

Administrator. It seemed that Ally McBeal's smoothly modulated heart-felt confessions on TV entranced her a lot more than what was going on in my own heart and mind. Strange and troubling how TV deflects from the dramas in our own families. I would have liked to talk to her about the past 10 years, but there never seemed a chance.

What kept me going was applying for a Radcliffe Fellowship to write about the psychic/supernatural voices and making my second solo CD, "Spell on You" with gospel/jazz pianist Geoffrey Dana Hicks. My first gig with the band, my jaw locked so badly that I was in agony and didn't think I could sing. When the band started to play, the performer in me just ran downstairs to the stage with the saxophone player between me and the bandleader so he couldn't see my contorted face. I sang somehow with a locked jaw. Then I really understood that psychologically speaking, being 'home" was not where I'd become an artist, but New York City. I was banking on that Radcliffe Fellowship against the odds, up against Ph.Ds, and acclaimed published writers. It was, at best, a controversial topic. The voices had left me then, but I still felt that their entrance into my life had been a major spiritual event and an importantly weird phenomenon to explore as a writer.

By March my three months were up. I'd been notified that I was rejected for the Fellowship, but was in the throes of recording "Spell on You." I worked some miserable temp jobs to survive and used my disability money to finish the record. I finally gave up my studio in NY when my subletter got behind in the rent and wound up in housing court. Cruella DaVille, the harsh Russian woman who lived out in Brooklyn from where she managed the E. Village apartment building, tried to buy her off to move and get rid of me for good. It was technically an illegal sublet. So, I lost the studio on Ave. A. There was no concrete tie left then to the City; my bridge back had been burned.

Freddie went back to his steadfast girlfriend/angel of many years, Colleen, a car insurance salesman who worked in neighboring Swampscott and who had refurbished a house they could share. Freddie called me up one day and said, "You have your music and I need Colleen." The final straw was standing me up on my birthday on a date to have dinner in the North End at "Catch of the Day." At least, I later wrote a blues about it called, "Birthday."

"You left me on my birthday
flames around the cake
I danced like a Madonna
You bit me like a snake…."

I started writing again and got my own place. And fortuitously a band I'd had in NYC called, "Leda's Swan" was revived when I visited my friend and drummer from the Bronx, Will DiMartino. Then my poetry collection "Hot Rain" got published by Ibbetson St. Press after a fairy goddess in a small art gallery recommended me to a publisher on the scene. So, did it all work out? Or hadn't the shrink in NY really been right? Stay in NYC and fight, she had suggested. Probably, she was right. But once I'd made the move back to Boston, I couldn't seem to peel myself away, especially at a time when the E. Village was becoming more and more expensive, more and more the hedonistic playground for trust fund kids, Wall Street brokers and New Jersey pleasure seekers on the weekends. Not that I didn't miss the mystical little parks on the Lower East Side, running by the East River, the crazy cultural hustle and wild stimulation of the hood. To me Boston was still provincial and old world; New York was the badlands. And there were those roses at 4 a.m. always being freshly cut and arranged at the Korean deli on my corner .... I thought of those often.

Had I simply lost my guts? Had my will become as paralyzed as my jaw that night when I had to sing at the restaurant?

Maybe artists never have a real home. Maybe their home is in their creations anyway.

What I also realized strangely is this: as much as his charisma and bravery and the sex—which did take away my pain and depression in bursts like a narcotic itself—Freddie was really a stand in for my dead Italian father and my estranged brother. But it just doesn't work out that way. Because poet Rene Char may write, "There is no absence that cannot be replaced," but I always doubted this to be true. No, it is a bad idea. Freddie was a demon, was Freddie. Once you leave home you've changed, you've changed, you've changed.

So how do I make my peace with being back? Do the gold-dust and the night tattoos of Gotham City ever re-emerge? Or are they gone forever? How does my perspective keep shifting, as it needs to, in a place that seems ghostly and fixed?

Well, I have labored, sinned, and somehow as karma would have it, paid for it. And here I am tonight by the Charles River. There are spirits in the cobalt sky. I can feel the crosswinds of history from the Puritans and their wintry God of perseverance to the founding of Harvard College…1/3 of the men in Massachusetts served in the Civil War under President Lincoln… North vs. South because of the enslavement of Africans, their agony, cakewalks and blues, because of tribalisms and economics. Then my father's immigration with many Italians and Irish at the turn of the century. Factories, bridges and trolleys were constructed. I was raised on the lore of politics—of Kennedys and Kings.

> "History is an angel blown backwards by the future. History is a pile of debris. And the angel wants so to go back and fix things. To repair what has been broken. But there's a storm blowing from paradise, Blowing the angel backwards, into the future. And that storm, that storm, is called, progress…."

Laurie Anderson, The Dream Before "Strange Angels," I remember those lyrics again as if I were channeling them. Those lyrics impacted me like a sword of truth the first time I heard them from a woman whose voice induced me to stop acting and try and become a songwriter and vocalist. And in them is that notion of progress. It's blowing the angel backwards in a storm. Is progress, if we keep going, somehow inevitable?

My lost lovers' names blow across the face of the moon's breath, as the dark banks of the night are lit up by Buckingham Street. And with starry sweat on my face and the wind in my hair, I can hear those voices that have haunted me for years cut their mesmerizing mantras across the sky and into the river's rushes…

Tonight I feel rooted in this place. So here I am. Here I am in this place that most people would call my home. Here I am back in Boston. Here I am anyway.

§

*Eleanor Goodman*

## Piety

I watch him struggle
over simple things —

refilling a water glass
as though he might spill
and break a hip.

Phantom pains,
fears of snowstorms, cancer, dogs.
Worry strips his layers off

reveals a folded corner
waiting to unfurl, hides the younger face
a proud San Francisco hippie

holding me out to the camera
my face red and squalling, and his smile
hidden behind a wispy beard

that embarrassed us both.
He shaved it the year I turned twelve,
when he said I was smarter

than Kelly Randall, my sixth grade rival,
and not to care about her teasing.
It will pass.

But I shut my bedroom door
and wouldn't play along
when he sang Hallelujah I'm a Bum
folding clothes in the basement
I held back
until even my socks
were too personal to show.
Forgive me.
Forgive me.

I have doled out love
with teaspoons
while he has done nothing but pour.

collection of Anne Brudevold

*Judith Barrington*

## The Salmon

She creams the water with her tail,
shoots back to the sandy bank
where she laid her eggs and wards
off intruders, this grizzled daughter of kings.

Already, the great spotted male
with his crusty back has touched her flank
and flung his milky magic toward
the nest, a cloud drifting and clinging

to globes of new life. She grows frail
and drifts, swaying as if a little drunk;
taken by the current from her precious hoard
she'll ground downstream where the kingfisher sings.

Will her dying eye see the eagle sail
onto the cedar high above? Now she's his mark—already
destined to be lifted by this new lord
into an airy world of waterless things.

*Abbott Ikeler*

## 507 North Broadway

Every summer in the fifties we came for a couple of weeks out of Pennsylvania's wrinkled hills west and south past motor courts and cornfields and rhyming roadside ads for Burma-Shave. Steubenville, Zanesville, Chillicothe: down across Ohio's heart in the murderous heat, heading for Kentucky. Most years we did it in a single, twelve-hour drive, tobacco billboards and derelict farm buildings giving way near the end to horses pasturing behind white fences, freshly painted.

With few exceptions, it was a pilgrimage my mother and I made to her mother's house alone, coasting into Lexington in a rattling second-hand Buick that startled the thoroughbreds from their grazing.

The house itself, even from the outside, didn't belong there. Didn't, I've often thought since, belong then either. Beyond the front walk, overgrown with rhododendrons, a fan doorway was just visible between thick white columns reaching to the third story roof. Around behind, the tangled riot of an English garden grew at will, its narrow jungly paths interrupted by sundials, birdbaths, hummingbird feeders and the tombstone of a dog. The inscription read "Winnie, 1936-1954."

For a boy growing up in Eisenhower's America, things got even stranger inside. Relatives, poor or otherwise, were greeted in the front hall by a British housekeeper, once the governess—Miss Hurley by name. White-haired, hardly five feet tall, with the posture of a sergeant major and a quite intimidating bosom, Miss Hurley was in charge of visitors. To me she seemed always to march rather than walk: her voice sharp, her lips pursed, her eyes unblinking, her attitude on all occasions brusque. She was especially skilled at telling children what to do and freezing them into compliance. I was no match for her, even when I outgrew her by a foot.

The interior of the house reinforced my awe. The entrance hall was paneled oak, two stories high, weighted in the corners with great blocks of mahogany furniture. A broad staircase at the back ran up from right to left. Under the stairs a low door cut in the paneling led to a secret room, hardly more than a crawl space, where Miss Hurley kept rewards for good boys and girls—sweets and Coke and ginger beer.

Another door at the back of the hall, with an inset square of glass, was the central mystery in grandmother's house. With a sharp pull, it opened on crisscrossing diagonals of wrought iron. They accordioned back and let me into what I'm sure was the smallest elevator in the world—a kind of dumbwaiter for one person. When I pressed the single button inside (which I did as often as Miss Hurley would let me), it lifted me first with a jolt and then with agonizing slowness to the second floor. To me it was an inexplicable presence in the house, the reality of which I felt obliged to check several times a day.

There were other peculiarities about the place: deserted servants' quarters up the backstairs and, in all the bedrooms, an ancient communications system of speaking tubes and switches that stubbornly refused to carry voices no matter how I shouted or pressed my ear to the brass openings in the wall. And in my mother's room and mine, always the mild, ineffable aroma of dried rose petals coming from jars on mantels, dressers, and bedside tables.

Miss Hurley and these oddities of architecture played their part to be sure, but it was chiefly my grandmother herself who convinced me that in entering her house I had stepped into the past.

To begin with, her notions of the parent-child relation were those of the English gentry before the First World War. It probably didn't help that she was the widow of an Episcopal bishop, educated at Oxford when Victoria was queen. We met four times, formally, each day: breakfast, luncheon, and supper in the dining room, and four o'clock tea in the sitting room just behind. At every meal grandmother, past seventy and portly, sat at the table's head, Miss Hurley at the foot, each with a sterling silver bell at her right hand to call the maid or cook.

Breakfast was a difficult passage for me.

Grandmother apparently believed quite fervently that unsweetened oatmeal, swimming in milk, was a particular favorite of little boys. One look at her gray-blue eyes (and her interminable aquiline nose) silenced any thoughts I had of contradiction. If porridge would not make me happy, she occasionally offered me grandfather's first choice: an egg cooked as he liked it, just three minutes. That it was raw and barely warm—and that grandfather had died well before my second birthday—seemed to matter to no one in that house. On the contrary, it appeared only to inspire a fiercer adherence to his tastes.

Afternoon tea was an easier affair. The four of us sat on amply stuffed furniture overlooking the garden and the hummingbirds. Miss Hurley brought the service on a brass tray accompanied by ginger cookies. Grandmother herself poured for us all, carefully doling into the dark, bitter, leafy brew the extravagant quantities of cream and sugar I demanded. She managed to convey a sense of quite intense importance to the ritual: something akin, in the gravity of her gestures, to the distribution of communion wafers.

On one occasion, her heart expanded (in the glow of my enjoyment of a second cup and several cookies) to an invitation to play cards. My mother and Miss Hurley left me alone to learn in her august presence the intricacies of Old Maid. We sat opposite one another, the cards laid out between us on the circular tea tray. She was a patient teacher, correcting gently, praising me when I understood, enlarging my vocabulary of games with several hands of Solitaire and Rummy as well. We played in fact for hours, though our conversation was always about the cards. I felt then for the first time how much she wished to step over the shadow of her own propriety and connect to those she loved—and at the same time how immensely hard it was for her to do so.

On another occasion grandmother requested my single presence on the sun porch where she worked daily at her correspondence after breakfast. She put question upon question to me about my schoolwork and the games I liked and what I wished to be when I became a man. She faced me in a white wicker chair in the late morning light, pen in hand, invoking as often as she could my rarely used first name. I understood even then the reason why. It had been her husband's own.

Once, and once only, did I spend any time with my

grandmother outside her house. On one of our annual visits (I must have been seven or eight), she broke from her usual routine and announced a desire to take me to an afternoon movie in the city. Both my mother and Miss Hurley took pains to prepare me for the privilege, scrubbing me up as if for antiseptic surgery, instructing me to take grandmother's arm when crossing streets, and to behave in all respects like the young gentleman I was expected to be.

We met in the front hall precisely at one, my mother still straightening my tie and brushing lint from my Robert Hall suit. Grandmother came down in a navy blue polka dot dress, white gloves and a broad-brimmed summer hat, also navy blue, that cast her face entirely in shadow. She was obviously proud of the hat, adjusting it in the mirror several times before we left.

Miss Hurley opened the door and wished us, in her clipped and nasal accent, down the steps and on our way. We went out the low iron gate, walking right some fifty yards to a bus stop. Grandmother didn't drive, but she clearly knew which bus we should wait for, when the next one would arrive, and how much the fare was for a child. I remember my astonishment as we stood there, not so much at her familiarity with public transport, but at the simple fact that she was able to exist at all outside the very special climate of her house.

I was also dimly aware, as we stepped up into the bus and dropped the required coins in the fare box, that a point was being made about thrift and self-reliance. We could, after all, have easily taken a taxi. Half a dozen stops later we got off the bus opposite a tall, yellow-brick building. At right angles to the windows, a sign ran up its side announcing BIJOU in vertically arranged letters made of purple-painted light bulbs.

We crossed the intersection, arm in arm, in the bright August sun. What I remember of the outing stops there, like a freeze-frame: grandmother and I on a crowded street, walking toward the theater, having our adventure.

A few summers later the pattern of our visits changed. We stayed barely a week: grandmother had grown weaker and seldom left her room. Miss Hurley sat at the head of the table, ringing the servant's bell more often than grandmother had. No one played cards. Sometimes I was farmed out to an aunt and cousins in Louisville for all but a few days while my mother stayed on in the house. Bit by bit, I learned of grandmother's ailments: she had been giving herself insulin shots in the thigh every morning for forty years; she was growing increasingly forgetful, repeating the same news in letter after letter; ulcers on her legs refused to heal; she suffered from angina.

On our last trip to Lexington, she was not in the house at all. Mother spent an hour with her at the hospital every day, while I waited in the car, too young for visiting privileges, too frightened to be left behind.

The last time my mother saw her, she was in an oxygen tent, intravenous drips in her arms, electrodes across her chest. Near the end of their visit grandmother struggled to speak and motioned her to come close. According to my mother, she whispered, after some considerable effort, a single phrase: "This body of our humiliation." It didn't even sound like English to me then.

She died on Columbus Day, 1957. By her own count, she was a few days short of her seventy-seventh birthday. My mother and my aunt, suspecting she might be older than she claimed, stood outside the church on the day of the funeral, waiting for the bell to toll. In those days tradition dictated that it be rung once for every year the deceased had lived. As the coffin was carried up the steps and through the arched doorway, the ponderous rhythm began. The two women counted aloud, softly, together.

The bell rang eighty times.

§

*Llyn Clague*

## In the Subway

Jolted out of brooding
in a crowded subway car
over just-diagnosed prostate cancer—
"Excuse me," she said—
I looked up a wide red mouth
that bore a small smile
and clear hazel eyes.

She wriggled
into the cramped seat beside me
and we sat, hip to hip,
our bodies insulated
by coats, sweaters, shirts, pants...
still, I felt a knob of bone.

With my wife—my oath
of trust, my helpmeet
in sickness and in age—
on my other side,
wryly I think, oh yes,
and am I going to caress
the young skin on the near hand
graze the cheek right there
in this crowded car
with my wife on the other side?

Dropped back
into the tunnel of brooding,
I stare down the hard dark.
What if knife or radiation
saves my life
but leaves me soft...worse—
in a subway car
with my wife next to me
where I am not going to do anything—
uninterested?

Oh, I cry to the red smile,
You're welcome to sit beside me.
Very welcome. Please sit
right here.

Steve Glines

*Mara Marvel*

## Returning the Wolves Home

If you would bring the wolves home
Take the door off the hinges, let the snow
Sweep the carpets, let bats nest behind drapes
Welcome moss in all the holes

When we live our lives like wolves
Walking together yet deeply alone
When our souls clear so our hearts see
Then the wolves will come home

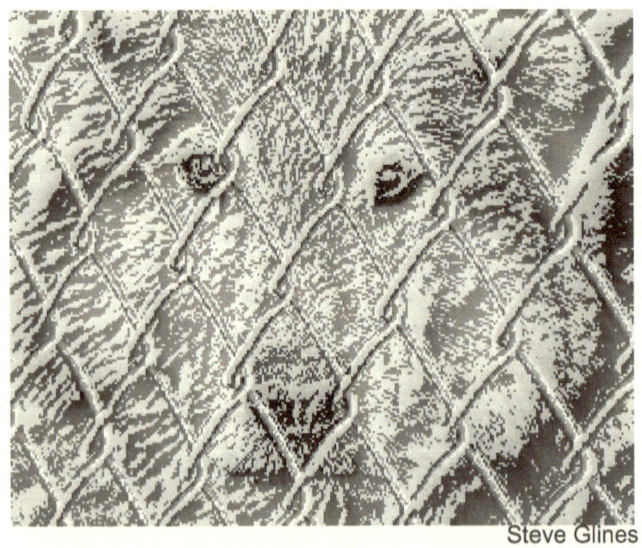

Steve Glines

*Ruth Sabath Rosenthal*

## Should I

urge my twin to live
in my agreeable domain
try to right the wrong
she felt coming in second—
do I want her to darken
my avenues with her ongoing complaints
and phobic-driven discontent—endless
fretting and time spent never
expressing even a modicum of joy
her pounds of flesh wasting
away days in front of a TV screen
or in snooze mode within earshot
of squawk-box scream—
me knocking myself
out trying to transmit optimism
I'll live to regret?

collection of
Katherine Adams

*Anne Brudevold*

## Photographs

In this one you are the grass
in this one you peer through a glass darkly
a faun in faun's skin
in this one you are dressed in velour
in a funeral parlour
in a great wooden casket
all the thoughts you've not thought
all the words you've not said
in this one you are me
in this one you were never meant to be
in this one you are the creak in the floor
in this one you are the hinge in the door
between the past and what could have been
if you had been in this one.

collection of
Anne Brudevold

Erik Iversen

*Paul Hotovsky*

## The Return

And I the discoverer
of my own childhood
named after me for my famous
explorations there
return for a stroll around
the old neighborhood.
I disembark at Taylor Park,
my ship steeply rocking
under a chestnut tree
in whose shade I am parked.
I walk down Ridgewood Road
reeling anachronistic and
majestic as Magellan
returning to view the narrows
and corners I uncovered
on my way up and out
to the Pacific. The little
streets shrink before me.
The houses cover their mouths
and stare. I stand before the house
that was my house once.

Suddenly a red sleeve
sticks out the door like a tongue,
retrieves the mail and is gone.
So I walk up Oval Road
and stand before the house
that was her house once.
Here the roundness of earth,
the softness of earth,
were first proved to me
beyond a doubt. But
here comes an old woman
dragging a garbage barrel out
to the curb. And she gives me
a queer look. I think it must be
the look the queen dowager gave
Magellan, when the handsome
young navigator asked her
only to believe that he believed
he could return without turning back.

*Lisa Igloria*

## Somnambula

All weekend I lie
clutching air to my side.   I slide
in and out of sleep, hearing

the thunder of teaspoons, the distant
whistle of a kettle boiling on the stove.
I struggle to wake, to read

at the desk and write, waiting
for the ceiling's tides to recede
and the floor to become

again its matted, boring hide.
Drifting back into dreams, I remember
a poet's lines about how, in the night,

each foot has nothing to love
but the other foot .  I think
about those mornings when we

turn back the blinds, when we
rehearse the knobs and fingers
laddering up and down the half,

the three-quarters of an hour,
at what point the catch
in our breaths turns
the flesh of midday supple.
How far back will it take
us, into that beginning

before either of us
even knew what we know
at this moment, before spinning

us back? The hammer and the heater
dull behind the walls.
A bracelet of sunlight falling

at an angle on the floor
is the day's small kindness,
its unmoved reminder.

collection of Anne Brudevold

*Karen D'Amato*

## Housekeeping

*(for my husband, Neil,*
*on the seventh anniversary*
*of my first husband's death)*

I don't know what I want
exactly. A neat house makes me sad.
It's like the one who's neat
is lonely and no one laughs there.

But when ours wears a trail
of your pocket change, your many
moment of undress, and pepper
cracker crumbs, an old
stab takes my breath.

This is not just about
picking up after you.
He too whirled the house
with how much I could lose.

You know those backrests called
"husbands"—he liked to sail his red one
across the room before sleep, while I
jumped at its landing's whap

and whatever it grazed
in the dark—my dear
plants and perfume glass
and papers. Mornings

I found it, toppled-
over drunk, and
plopped it on the pillows
of the new-made bed.

Though I chafed, he didn't
stop. And nothing broke.

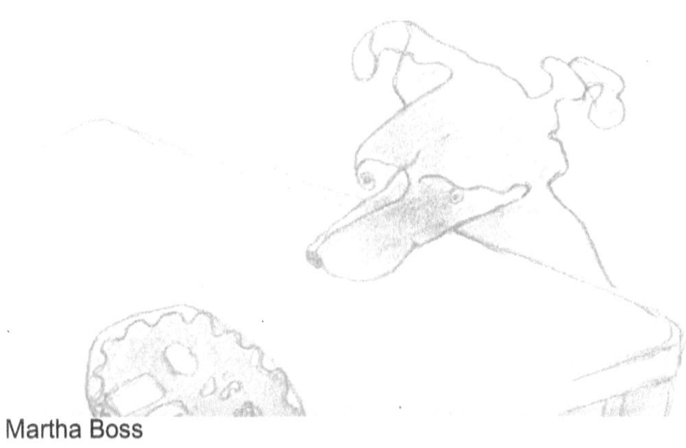

Martha Boss

*Barbara Lydecker Crane*

## Night Flight

Limbs tingle in half-remembered lightness.
All it takes is a small spring of knees,
arms spread wide on heft of air, just right.
I arch my supple spine to rise,
lift a shoulder if I choose to veer.
          Ah, the ease of flight!

Land unrolls below--a queen-sized quilt
patched in bright yards and dark rooftops,
threaded by a stream of silver light.
Yelping boys are running in a pack,
their arms upraised as if with strings to me,
          their tethered kite.

From high above the garden, the girls are a sight,
pinwheeling arms *Take me too! Take me too!*
I wave my outstretched hands, and sigh.
Soon enough, I'll feed their hungry faces
tipping toward me like woodland saplings
          into sunlight.

Farther along, I spot my Mom, tightly
grasping her walker. Every time I visit
she clutches my arm, leans in and confides
*I don't think I'll let you go.* I smile and shiver.
Dutiful daughter, I call, but she's deaf to me
          at this height.

Sun is setting now, mountains mauve in twilight.
There's my hiker husband, beaming
on this choose-your-own-adventure night.
He doesn't see me yet. I'll barnstorm
prickly pines to give a glancing
          kiss goodnight.

My limbs grow goose-bumps in moonlight.
It must be time to circle back
to home's warm bed. I will alight
without a sound: no one will know
I was gone, alone and soaring,
          out-of-bounds tonight.

*Jessica Harman*

## Cyan

Books piled on wicker shelves that I found
thrown-out- I'm a scavenger- dried flowers
in bottles melting with red candle-wax,
a feel of talking late into the night. The mirrors

always hold early evening
light. I am home among the bright slats slanting
from Venetian blinds that look onto the alleyway
of cool colors: always the same

quiet gray dust pools itself into cooling leaves.
Summer's freshness blazes into fall, that season
when I come home
from the odyssey— you looked at me,

I felt you looking—but there was nothing
I could say to explain this. I put on
my coat with buttons the color of autumn.
The lucky sense of vertigo welled

up in the sky—until you, I was heavily into muted
blues, like my bedspread of dove
gray, like a city I remember of fabric
stores that were mysteriously always

closed, the bolts of dark cloth dusty
with daytime moonlight. There, there were cool
candle-lit tones in otherwise warm-toned
restaurants with sidewalk terraces. There was

garbage on the streets, ice cream names
in different languages and church bells made
of cold music—but you taught me to see
the palest bluest blues, the cyans, the clarity
here in this little trembling place I call my new city.

*Lisha Adela Garcia*

## Breathing Forward in America

James is the Americanized name
of my D.C. cabbie, who fled soil-starved
Nigeria, to drive me to the Hyatt from the airport.
The militias that killed his wife and children missed
him as he had gone to Lagos for work.

The angels say we imprint our path
before we arrive as babies. I chose stones
slung across my back in guilt.

Camdelaria who cleans my toilet at the hotel,
came from El Salvador. She is a doctor.
Better a half-life with little dignity in work
than the scripts of violence tattooed on her flesh.

Their nightmares live in screams
I don't hear. Survival
memories are headstones
dedicated to savagery.

Music, what remains of their attempts?
to breathe forward in America. James' long
fingers tap the steering wheel to a tune
in a language I never heard.

Candelaria sways with a Mijares ballad
as she vacuums. I want
to believe my hand is free
of any nails I might have hammered
into their flesh but I know this cannot be true.

*Bernadette Davidson*

## Love Song for Roxbury

Puerto Rican flags fly, flicker.
Souped-up cars cruising School street
salsa erupting, sparkle, smoke, tailpipes hanging.

Corn braided child hopscotchs,
book bag bouncing behind.
Head-wrapped woman sways on stairs,
hips rocking, cloth bags swinging, on weary shoulders.

Wind chimes clang, while blue virgins in bathtubs
preside over pin wheels, bird baths, flamingos, flowers.
On crumbling porches families light citronella,
clink sangria, kool-aid, gin, while folks play cards, laugh and curse.

At the laundry on Washington
the Santiago family puzzles
over American washing machines
loading too much soap that spills on the floor.

A Vietnamese peddler carries pirate CDs,
wheels and deals bartering
in English, Spanish, Vietnamese,
falling back on gesture when all else fails.

*Jaques Fleury*

## Dancing Queen, Where You at?

*for Nneka, my graceful and thoughtful DIVA*

Dancing Queen, where you at?
the music is still blazing
last time we saw you
your legs were bleeding
in those parts, melancholy is crying
her face swollen with tears
dancing queen, where you at?
splinters of our hears
are breaking apart
the color of our rainbow is stuck on blue
a flock of birds still chirps softly above our heads
waiting hungry to be fed
our starry skies have diminished in size
dancing queen, where you at?
if you come we won't disgrace you
we tried but we never could replace you
in the twilight hour our moon will crown you
as you twirl in the bitter mountain winds the music
will wish you wings then you will release your swing
hip hip hooray!
our shadows will speak!
grateful that you'll have made us complete
we will welcome you back
in very familiar zones
but hurry before our dancing shoes have turned to stones!
come dance with us!
dancing queen, where you at?

*Harris Gardner*

## Mother's Universal War Cry

"Wait 'til your father gets home!"
Mother's sword of Damocles,
that juvenile threat of paternal damnation.

"Wait 'til your father gets home!"
I'm in for it, no question.
Never should have tried the shingle roof

for a makeshift slide. Never mind
the palms full of splinters, when palms
and feet are brakes that keep you

from falling off the edge.
This great rush sweeter than sledding downhill
with your wizard brother and sister.

Now you are about to face the wrath
of your father, if not Heaven, too.
He labors like Sisyphus to support the house.

Oh, the Jewish guilt! So well remembered,
so ill endured. This 1950's family,
so rooted and held up with structure.

"Baa baa black sheep have you any wool?"
I could have answered that question
Nobody asked. Grounded again.

*Penny Harter*

## Sometimes Late at Night

sometimes late at night
when the dark lifts me from my bed
I float in it,
and all the bodies of my life—
my own, yours
the dear shape of my parents over dinner
the sturdy flesh of my children—
seem insubstantial
floating beside me in that dark,
gone to smoke or mist.

Even this planet,
rolling through the greater dark
where gaseous fires sputter
and go out, grows wraith-like
a hologram I poke my finger through
as I drift beside it
unable to find my way home
because home doesn't matter anymore
because home makes a sound like the wind.

UNITED STATES
OF AMERICA

War Ration Book One

No. 343839 -294

WARNING

1 Punishments ranging as high as *Ten Years' Imprisonment or $10,000 Fine, or Both*, may be imposed under United States Statutes for violations thereof arising out of infractions of Rationing Orders and Regulations.

2 This book must not be transferred. It must be held and used only by or on behalf of the person to whom it has been issued, and anyone presenting it thereby represents to the Office of Price Administration, an agency of the United States Government, that it is being so held and so used. For any misuse of this book it may be taken from the holder by the Office of Price Administration.

3 In the event either of the departure from the United States of the person to whom this book is issued, or his or her death, the book must be surrendered in accordance with the Regulations.

4 Any person finding a lost book must deliver it promptly to the nearest Ration Board.

OFFICE OF PRICE ADMINISTRATION

*Katherine Adams*

## Imposing Stature

Greenville was a typical small southern town for 1958. We moved there that year when I was five years old. With a population of about 15,000, the town was proud of its 45 churches. The one Catholic church was looked upon as "different" — a euphemism for suspicious and inferior. Some people made it their business to know where the Catholics lived. The town was completely segregated back then. There was a black experience of life and a white one and they were worlds apart. Once, I remember asking someone what was noteworthy about the town. The answer was Tripp's Warehouse which was the largest tobacco warehouse in the world. Since Greenville was incorporated around the 1900's, it didn't have any Civil War history. But, you wouldn't know it by the way everyone acted — rebel flags proudly displayed from houses and cars and hats. People opened football games with a rousing "Dixie." (The other, obligatory anthem was always given a conspicuously lackluster airing.)

From the beginning, we were looked upon as outsiders. First of all, my parents were both English professors at the college up the street. That made us "college people" which was cause for mistrust. Second, since I had no brothers and sisters, this made me an "only child," which meant afflicted in addition to different. An introduction from one mother to another was often "This is Katherine. She's an [pause] [speaking slowly, half whispering] 'only' child." I knew the lingering sideways glance through narrowed eyes meant that judgment had been passed. I was ashamed but didn't know why.

The perceived peculiarities of my family until now were on a small scale. What was to come made our idiosyncrasies look like church-going — which we didn't do either.

About a year after we moved to this eastern North Carolina town, my parents acquired a certain piece of sculpture that required considerable adjustment on the part of some townspeople. My parents had bought an eight-foot high statue that weighed about 500 pounds. Up to this point, our back yard was home to a gas tank, weeping willow, honeysuckle hedge and a toad. Now the statue occupied dead center. This was no ordinary eight-foot tall statue, if indeed there can be one in a backyard. This was a black cement statue of a nude woman. A strong, stretching and sensual woman. There she stood — her spectacle of public nudity an affront to the prevailing Christian sense of modesty. She became one of the more entertaining topics of conversation.

Everyone had a reaction. The neighborhood dogs shied away from it. As one of my friends said years later, "within two weeks of you all getting that statue the whole town knew about it." Move over ordinary backyard, move over semblance of a typical childhood, move over Tripp's Warehouse. I had no idea when my parents brought home that statue that my fate had been sealed. My role would require armor I did not yet have.

My parents never intended to offend people. They were not easily scandalized themselves and roundly dismissed what they saw as people's ignorant attitudes. They were very secure in their idea of private property and nobody's business. They cultivated their interests, which included art and entertaining. My parents' friends all took the statue in stride. They appreciated it as a work of art, and as support of a local artist. The irony of it in a southern backyard wasn't lost on them either.

The social circles of my parents didn't include many native folks, but mine did. These people—whom I liked and who liked me—were curious about the statue. As a tomboy roaming around the neighborhood, I was often asked for an explanation of it. Bunches of little boys would make pilgrimages to our backyard to gaze up at it. At school, they would come up to me at recess and ask, "How come you have that statue of a nekk-id lady in your backyard?"

My parents drank alcohol and they gave parties. Their guests would often go out into the yard and gather around the statue. Drinking in private, being much less visible, wasn't so awful, but blatant consumption of alcohol was looked upon as sinful and depraved by most of the townspeople. And there they all were—consuming heartily, carousing happily, beside the statue who was being naked with a vengeance. I had gone to Bible School with a friend and I had heard about Sodom and Gomorrah. Unwittingly, I spread the word. I didn't realize that bringing my lunch to school in paper bags shaped to hold fifths of liquor would be a bad idea. When I was singled out for misbehaving at school, teachers would give me that interminable, icy look of disapproval. When the teachers did manage to verbalize something it was not helpful and usually included the word "unladylike." I was again setting an example of impropriety that I was confused about. I countered them with an outer pride even though inside I hurt and longed to be invisible.

But, in spite of my young age, I had moments of insight regarding this unique situation. There were times of clarity when I knew that straddling these two worlds was a rare opportunity and felt lucky because of it. Every Sunday morning my parents and I would drive down to the newsstand together to pick up the "New York Times." On this day of the week practically everyone was in church and at this hour most churches had just let out, their congregations spilling onto the sidewalks. We would drive by at least a few of these crowds (and they were crowds back then) on our way to get the papers. Daddy would remark with enthusiastic irreverence, "Look at all the Christians!" "There they all are," Mother would idly respond, slowly saying each word and inflecting the last with a higher pitch. "We're out among 'em!" Daddy would say, with joking alarm. Then he'd catch my eye in the rearview mirror and with mock seriousness raise his fist, "Courage!" "Chin up!" he'd rally. Humor released tension and at that moment living in two disparate worlds was something fascinating, rewarding and, for a few moments, perfectly balanced.

In 1968, when I was 15, we moved to Virginia. It seemed so long ago that I had dreams of the statue chasing me up the slide. Thankfully, in that house, it could fit inside. But anyway, times had changed.

Regardless, people haven't forgotten. Old, out-of-touch friends never fail to ask with intense curiosity and a bit of nostalgia, "... Do your parents still have that statue?"

§

Katherine Adams

*Helen Bar-Lev*

## To Discover Home

An error of the Fates
and you are born
in a place alien to your soul
and you know it from infanthood
when everything in your path
is an obstacle,
even the language is difficult
and customs seem odd,
behaviour strange,
food unpalatable,
you suffer from the weather,
and feel you are observing it all
on a confused movie screen

And then you chance
to travel to a promised land
where the sun glows gold
the greens appeal
flowers are perfection
speech resonates friendly
habits please
food is ambrosia
bodies speak your language
temperatures suit your body
language is learned instantly

You wonder if sometimes
the Fates have no insight
into the soul's needs,
leaving you to discover everything
on your own
(or was it the Fates,
realizing their mistake,
who guided you out of the mess
in which they originally placed you?)

Never mind,
you've come home
the past is forgotten
the Fates are forgiven
and life goes on
exactly as it should

Martha Boss

*Judith Barrington*

## The Questionnaire

Somebody printed a five-page questionnaire
to find out how animals felt about life in the zoo.
They asked: "Where is home?" and "Do you know
how to get there?"

They ran down the list with a monkey, they grilled
a black bear,
but they got no response, except for a grunt from the gnu,
and the moose simple chewed up the five-page questionnaire

so they started again, determined to be more aware.
"We mean you no harm," they said, "you surely once knew—
so can't you remember your home and how you might
get there?"

"Perhaps it's the language," they thought: "since they come
from elsewhere"
so they called in translators; tried Swedish and Greek and Hindu
but still no response to the five-page questionnaire:

the whole hippo tribe appeared to be deep in prayer
while badger was much too depressed, and the
elderly shrew
just spat when they mentioned her home and
how she could get there.

That might have been it—the end of the silly affair
but an elephant standing nearby spoke up: "Hey you,"
she bellowed, "to hell with your five-page questionnaire.
*Just tell me* where home is. Tell me: how do I get there?"

Anne Brudevold

## Contributor Notes

KATHERINE ADAMS lives in Brookline, MA., teaches meditation instruction and is the mother of a 16 year old.

HOLLY ANDERSON is anthologized in Up is Up, But So is Down: New York's Downtown Library, Scene, (1974-1992 (NYU Press 2006,) Unbearables (Autonomedia 1995,) Lily Lou (Purgatory Pie Press 1986,) and Scheherazade (1988.) She is published in magazines Rampike, Raddle Moon, Redtape, Benzene, Conduit.

HELEN BAR-LEV's poems and paintings have appeared in The Other Voices International Project; The Coffee Press Journal; Boheme Magazine; The Poetry Bridge; Sketchbook; River Bones Press; The Hypertexts; Palabras-Press; and Poetry Super Highway, and print anthologies Meeting of the Minds Journal; Voices Israel Anthologies; Manifold Magazine of New Poetry (U.K.); Lucidity Poetry Journal, Across The Long Bridge and Sailing in the Mist of Time. For Loving Precious Beast, Ibbetson Street 21 and The Rogue Scholars. A book entitled CYCLAMENS AND SWORDS with poems of Israel by Helen and Johnmichael Simon has been published by Ibbetson Press of Boston, Mass. and may be ordered from the authors hbarlev@netvision.net.il It is also available via Lulu. Her watercolor paintings and sketches are featured throughout the book. Helen is a member of Voices Israel English Poetry Society and Canadian Poetry Association. She is the global correspondent in Israel for the Poetry Bridge and Editor-in-Chief of the Voices Israel annual Anthology.

JUDITH BARRINGTON is the author of three volumes of poetry, most recently Horses and the Human Soul (Story Line Press, 2004.) Lifesaving: A Memoir was the 2000 winner of the Lambda Book Award and the PEN/Martha Albrand Award. She teaches across the U. S. and in Britain. Her website http://www.judithbarrington.com

BARBARA BECKWITH writes essays on everything from squash (the sport) to cataracts (as in eyes and flash floods), to family relations (from in-laws to grandchildren), to racism (in well-meaning white people) that appear in newspapers such as the New York Times and Christian Science Monitor, magazines including New Age and Yoga Journal, and anthologies including Gifts of the World (Seal Press) and Whatever It Takes: Women's on Women's Sport (FSG)

BARBARA BIALICK has published as a journalist in The Boston Globe, The Detroit News, Pittsburgh Magazine, New Age, McCalls and Whole Life Times. She published poetry in Lilith, Pemmican Press, Poetica, Jewish Currents, The Mid-American Poetry Review, Tucumcari and The Somerville News.

MARTHA BOSS is an artist and writer. She lives in Boston.

ANNE BRUDEVOLD:has taught writing at UMASS Amherst, Westfield State College, Holyoke Community College, and SUNY Stonybrook. She was co-poetry editor of journal Peregrine. Her poetry and fiction have been accepted in Poets On:, Onthebus, Windhorse, Small Pond, Pleaides, Black Bough, Mississippi Review, Bagelbards Anthology #2 (available at Amazon and Lulu), Ibbetson Street 21, Wilderness House Literary Review, Insight and Sacred Fools. A poem is pending in online Spoonful. Wilderness House Literary Review is publishing a serial version of her novel Hunter Moon, and has published Chapter 3 in the First Anthology, available at Lulu and Amazon. She was runner up for Best Short Story in The Optimist, a newspaper of Western MA. She is the editor of Eden Waters Press.

PHILIP BURNHAM's poems have appeared in Atlanta, Margie and Lyric. He has three published books, My Neighbor Adam, Sailing from Boston, and Housekeeping.

LLYN CLAGUE has six dozen poems published in Atlanta Review, Wisconsin Review, Mobius, Pegasus, The Iconoclast, Main Street Rag, The Aurorean, and Plainsong. His first book, Confessions, Selected and Edited is appearing in fall 2007 from Ibbetson Street Press. He was co-Managing Editor of Imprint.

BARBARA CRANE has poems in UU World, the Magazine of the Unitarian-Universalist Association, America, the National Catholic Weekly, and one forthcoming in 2008 Measure.

KAREN D'AMATO has been writing or dreaming about poetry for over twenty-five years and seeks to "live the poem." Currently a senior lecturer in English at Curry College, her work has appeared in the anthologies Grolier Poetry Prize 1998 and When a Lifemate Dies: Stories of Love, Loss, and Healing.

BERNADETTE DAVIDSON has been featured reader at many respected venues in the Boston area. She appears in Poetry Motel. She is an early childhood educator, directs programs in Boston's Chinatown, and teaches in several local universities.

DIANA DER-HOVANESSIAN, translator of Daniel Varoujan's poem, translated Varoujan poems for her father when he to give a lecture on Varoujan and wanted English versions. She later did nine volumes of Armenian translations, and one Romanian. She also has thirteen books of her own work, the last four published by Sheep Meadow Press.

IRIS JAMAHL DUNKLE has had work published in a number of online and print journals including Fence, Poetry Review, Poemeleon, SNReview, Kaleidowhirl, and The National Review. Currently she writes a column of poetry criticism for The Alsop Review.

JACQUES STANLEY FLEURY, a.k.a. "The Haitian Firefly" is a poet, freelance writer, journalist, columnist and Television show host. His work has been published widely in magazines around Boston, and he is well known for his readings at many venues. He is a tireless and no-holds-barred philosopher/activist/writer and net-worker. His website is haitianfirefly@yahoo.com.

JIM FORITANO has been writing poetry forever, though intermittently, and recently teaching modern literature to college freshmen and reviewing Boston area art exhibitions for Artscope magazine.

LO GALLUCCIO is a poet/writer and vocal artist from Cambridge MA and New York City. Her first chapbook of poems, "Hot Rain" was published by Singing Bone press in 2003. Published writing includes work in: Night magazine, I am from Lower East Side, Lungfull!, Ibbetston St. #15, 17 and 20, The Bagel Bard Anthology, Abramelin magazine, Strangeroad.com and the Wilderness Literary House Review. Her poem Millennium was nominated for a Pushcart Prize by Doug Holder of Ibbetson St. Press. In the spring of

2008, Cervena Barva Press will release a 70 page memoir entitled, "Sarasota VII". She credits prose-poetry writer Elizabeth Strand and novelist/filmmaker Marguerite Duras for inspiration in writing this unique & surreal work. She also serves as the Poetry Editor of the Cambridge Alewife and is a frequent reviewer for the Ibbetson Street Press. L. Anderson grants permission to quote from the "The Dream Before." www.logalluccio.com/
www.unofficiallogalluccio.atspace.com

LISHA ADELA GARCIA has a chapbook pending publication from Pudding House Press and a poem in the September issue of Crab Orchard Review. Her work is pending in anthologies Red hen Press and Bluelight Press. She is bilingual and bicultural. She lives in Arizona.

HARRIS GARDNER credits include The Jewish Advocate, The Harvard Review, Midstream, WHL Review, I Refused to Die-A Holocaust Study by Susie Davidson, and more than fifty other publications. He co-authored with Lainie Senechal Chalice of Eros. His most recent collection is Lest They Become (Ibbetson Street Press)2003. He hosts two poetry venues and was nominated for a Pushcart Prize—Fall, 2005. He won Honorable Mention in the Boyle-Farber Prize (New England Poetry Club) 2004.

STEVE GLINES, in addition to being the editor of Wilderness House Literary Review, is an essayist, journalist, storyteller, occasional poet, graphic designer and bon vivant. His motto is, "The best is barely good enough." Steve has published six books, only one of which might be considered even remotely "literary," a travelogue about Fiji. He has been published in Ibbitson Review, the Belmont Citizen, the Littleton Independent, Unix Review, Technology Review, the Boston Globe and the New York Times. He has never been published in the Paris Review, the AntiochReview, Crazyhorse, The Atlantic Monthly and the Kenyon Review. To these awesome credentials it should be added that he has never received a McArthur Award nor been nominated for a Pushcart or Pulitzer Prize. Still, for some reason, people like what he writes and, on occasion, pay him for it.

ELEANOR GOODMAN writes fiction and poetry and has published translations of Tang Dynasty Poetry. Her work has appeared in or is forthcoming in New Delta Review,

Seneca Review, The Pedestal Magazine and The Amherst Review. In 2007 she received an International Merit Award by the Atlanta Review. She teaches at Grub Street, a creative writing school in Boston.

JESSICA HARMAN, Brookline MA, has been a contributing editor of Matrix magazine in Montreal, and a research assistant at Harvard Medical School. Her poetry, prose, and artwork have appeared in Stand, Orbis, and Matrix. She published a chapbook in England in 2006 and has an essay on poetics forthcoming in The Iconoclast.

PENNY HARTER'S most recent books are The Night Marsh (forthcoming from Word Tech Editions, 2008), Along River Road (From Here Press, 2005,) and Lizard Light: Poems from the Earth (Sherman Asher books, 1998.) Her website is http://penhart.home.att.net.

DOUG HOLDER has two new collections of poetry out: "Of All the Meals I had Before," (Cervana Barva Press) and "No One Dies at the Au Bon Pain (sunnyoutside.) He wrote the introduction to Robert Lowell's Walking in the Blue in Robert Pinsky's anthology America's Favorite Poems.

PAUL HOTOVSKY works in Boston as an interpreter for the Deaf. His poetry appears widely online and in print. His website is www.paulhostovsky.com.

LUISA A. IGLORIA is an Associate Professor in the MFA Creative Writing Program and Department of English, Old Dominion University (Norfolk, Virginia). has published nine books including ENCANTO (Anvil, 2004), IN THE GARDEN OF THE THREE ISLANDS (Moyer Bell/ Asphodel, 1995), and TRILL & MORDENT (WordTech Editions, fall 2005)

ABBOTT IKELER teaches communications at Emerson College in Boston. His published work includes literary criticism, communication studies, poetry, and prose reminiscences, including a book on Thomas Carlyle, Puritan Temper and Transcendental Faith and a collection of poems, Outpost.

ERIK IVERSEN is finishing his second year of veterinary school in New Zealand. He likes to draw and photograph.

BIRGIT KVAMME LUNDHEIM lives in Trondheim, Norway, where she works as a painter. She has had solo exhibitions in Norway, Switzerland, and France. Two of her poems have been published in Spectrum Literary Arts Magazine.

TARA MARVEL has been hiking and writing in New Hampshire for over fifty years. Muskrat Stew, written with Penobscot elder, Fred Ranco, will be published by the University of Maine press in 2008. Her poems and illustrations have been published in journals and anthologies including Mountain Passages: An Appalachia Anthology. Her videopoems were screened at festivals in Europe. website at www.marvelousmedia.com.

ANDREA NICKI has had poetry published most recently in Stories of Women and Healing: Women Write the Body by Kent State University Press and the journal Rampike by Coach House Press.

JOYCE NOWER has a third book of poetry, The Qin Warriors and Other Poems, published by Avalanches Press. Her poetry and prose have appeared, or are scheduled to appear in Raven Chronicles, Earth's Daughters, The American Poetry Journal, Terminus, Slant, Visions-International, Avatar Review, Kaleidowhirl, and the National Poetry Council. She writes poetry criticism for The Alsop Review. Homepage: http://www.joycenower.com

CHAD PARENTEAU has been published in Main Street Rag, The November 3rd Club, Shampoo, and the anthology French Connections: A Gathering of Franco-American Poets. He hosts the Stone Soup Poetry series in Cambridge, MA every Monday night and edits the online journal Spoonful. (Http: stonesouppoetry.blogspot.com) His newest chapbook, Discarded, Poems For My Apartment is due out in 2008 from Cervena Barva Press.

PAM ROSENBLATT is an arts contributor for The Somerville News. Her poetry has appeared in Lyrical Somerville (The Somerville News), The Bagel Bards Anthology II and the Wilderness House Literary Review. She has published poetry book review online in Ibbetson Street Update (Ibbetson Street Press).

RUTH SABATH ROSENTHAL is an NY poet, published in Connecticut Review, Ibbetson Street, Jabberwork Review, Long Island Quarterly, Mobius-The Poetry Magazine, Pacific Review and Voices Israel Anthology. On Oct. 15th (Ruth's birthday) 2006, her poem "on yet another birthday" was nominated for a "Pushcart" prize by Ibbetson St.

TOM SHEEHAN has painted his house five times, put on two roofs, and rebuilt a kitchen twice. He had a quad bypass in 1991. His knees hurt now, but he walked ten miles a day for ten years after the cardiologist said I don't know what you are doing, but keep it up, and the knee doctor eventually said whatever you're doing, you are abusing yourself. He is married to a hospice nurse and has six children, one deceased.

JAMES "BONES" TOMASELLI is a performance artist, musician and photographer. Visit him at http://www.myspace.com/James Tomaselli.

DANIEL VAROUJAN wrote and edited a magazine in Constantinople (Istanbul) in 1915 during World War I, when the Turks rounded up poets and writers and killed them. He was kept in prison for several months where he was allowed to write a notebook of poems. After his execution, his notebook was sold by a jailer to an Armenian priest and it was published in the United States about six years later.

LIZ WATSON is an Australian born divorced mother of three living in Lexington, MA. She started writing poetry in her teens. She has lived outside her homeland for fifteen years, and hopes to return. She is a year round swimmer at Walden Pond.

JILL WINKOWSKI is a freelance writer and writing teacher. She writes regularly for The Daily Press in New Port News, Virginia.

www.ingramcontent.com/pod-product-compliance
Lightning Source LLC
LaVergne TN
LVHW050940080826
845145LV00004B/1343

* 9 7 8 0 6 1 5 1 8 2 4 3 8 *